CAPTAIN AWESOME
and the NEW KID

By STAN KIRBY

Illustrated by
GEORGE O'CONNOR

LITTLE SIMON
New York   London   Toronto   Sydney   New Delhi

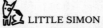 LITTLE SIMON

An imprint of Simon & Schuster Children's Publishing Division 1230 Avenue of the Americas, New York, New York 10020 Copyright © 2012 by Simon & Schuster, Inc. All rights reserved, including the right of reproduction in whole or in part in any form. LITTLE SIMON is a registered trademark of Simon & Schuster, Inc., and associated colophon is a trademark of Simon & Schuster, Inc. For information about special discounts for bulk purchases, please contact Simon & Schuster Special Sales at 1-866-506-1949 or business@simonandschuster.com. The Simon & Schuster Speakers Bureau can bring authors to your live event. For more information or to book an event contact the Simon & Schuster Speakers Bureau at 1-866-248-3049 or visit our website at www.simonspeakers.com. Manufactured in the United States of America 1013 MTN   10 9 8 7 6
Library of Congress Cataloging-in-Publication Data
Kirby, Stan. Captain Awesome and the new kid / by Stan Kirby ; illustrated by George O'Connor. — 1st ed. p. cm. Summary: Eugene McGillicudy stands up for Sally Williams, the new student at Sunnyview Elementary, and then discovers that they both like an orange cat named Mr. Whiskersworth and the comic book super hero, Super Dude. [etc.] [1. Superheroes—Fiction. 2. Friendship—Fiction. 3. Schools—Fiction. 4. Cats—Fiction.] I. O'Connor, George, ill. II. Title. PZ7. K633529Caf 2012 [Fic]—dc23 2011023400
ISBN 978-1-4424-4199-6 (pbk)
ISBN 978-1-4424-4200-9 (hc)
ISBN 978-1-4424-4201-6 (eBook)

Table of Contents

"RUN!"

Captain Awesome grabbed the Frisbee and raced for his life!

"We're not going to make it!" Nacho Cheese Man shouted, an empty can of cheese in his hand.

ROWWWWWL!

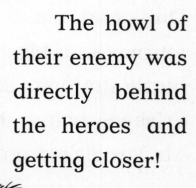

The howl of their enemy was directly behind the heroes and getting closer!

The Danger-Stopping Dynamic
Duo had made the dangerous
journey into Mr. Drools's Dog Star
battle station to save their precious
Frisbee being held captive in
Mr. Drools's drippy, droolish jaws.

What's that? you say. You've never heard of **Mr. Drools?** He's only the most slobberingest monster from the Howling Paw Nebula! He wakes up neighborhoods around the galaxy with his barking, his Drool of Destruction, and his taste for Frisbees.

What's that? you say again. Who are **Captain Awesome** and **Nacho Cheese Man?!**

Only the two most awesomest heroes not named Super Dude.

Super Dude just happened to be *the* most awesome superhero in Eugene's comic book collection.

Eugene McGillicudy and his best friend, Charlie Thomas Jones, were not just ordinary students at Sunnyview Elementary. They also had supersecret superhero identities: Eugene was Captain Awesome and Charlie was Nacho Cheese Man.

Along with Captain Awesome's hamster sidekick, Turbo, together

they formed the Sunnyview Superhero Squad to protect the universe from bad guys.

Especially drooling space dogs.

Captain Awesome and Nacho Cheese Man had landed the

Awesome Rocket on Mr. Drools's dreaded Dog Star—a grrrnormous battle station, shaped like a dog's head—that flew around the universe barking at helpless planets.

Boarding the Dog Star was the start of a three-part mission to save Eugene's favorite Frisbee.

The three parts were:

1. find the Frisbee

2. rescue the Frisbee, and

3. do not get drooled on by Mr. Drools! GROSS!

"GRRRRR!" Mr. Drools growled, drool squirting from his clenched teeth.

DOUBLE YUCK!

"Let's go!" shouted Captain Awesome, using his superspeed power to run through the long hallway of the Dog Star and nearly stepped on something lumpy. A scary thought jumped into Captain Awesome's head.

"Oh no! We're right in the middle of a Doggy Doo-Doo Minefield!" he shouted out to Nacho Cheese Man.

ICK!

A Doggy Doo-Doo Minefield was a scary *and* icky thought. Mr. Drools's Dog Star was full of traps! Very smelly traps . . .

"I'll stop the monster!" shouted Nacho Cheese Man. He grabbed a new can of power cheese from

his Cheese Bag
so he could aim
it at Mr. Drools.

PFSZZT!

Cheese blasted Nacho Cheese Man right in the face!

"Aargh!" he cried out. "I'm cheesed!"

Nacho Cheese Man had forgotten the first rule of the power of canned cheese: Point the can away from you.

"Mmmmm. It's yummy though!"

But it was not a time for snacks, no matter how yummy. Mr. Drools was within slobber range of the Frisbee. There was only one thing Captain Awesome could do.

WHIZZZ!

Captain Awesome threw the Frisbee to Nacho Cheese Man. Unfortunately, Nacho Cheese Man's face was still covered in gooey cheese. The Frisbee sailed over his head and Mr. Drools took off after it.

"The Frisbeeeeeeee!" cried out Captain Awesome.

"I'm on it!"

Nacho Cheese Man had his own Plan B: a Squeaky Dinky Squeezo. He pulled the doggie toy from his Cheese Bag and said the one word that no inhabitant of the Howling Paw Nebula could ever resist:

"FETCH!"

The Squeaky Dinky Squeezo worked! Mr. Drools took off after it.

"Good thinking, Nacho Cheese Man!" Captain Awesome exhaled. He was relieved.

"I learned from the best,"Nacho Cheese Man said, looking at his Super Dude watch. Super Dude had faced a similar situation in Super Dude No. 48 with The Kitty Litterer, The Cat That Littered. Super Dude had defeated her by using a giant ball of string.

While Mr. Drools dribbled his evil spittle on poor Squeaky Dinky, Captain Awesome grabbed the Frisbee and ran with Nacho Cheese Man toward the Dog Star airlock.

"MI-TEE!" Captain Awesome cried out and hopped onto his MI-TEE Mobile rocket bike and blasted away from the Dog Star. Nacho Cheese Man followed on his own rocket bike, The Cheesy Rider.

"Cheesy-Yoooo!" he cried as he took off.

But fast on their trail was
Mr. Drools, barking and drooling
as he chased after the boys.
Time for the Boomway!
They turned their rocket bikes
onto the Boomway, the outer

space bike path. Captain Awesome pushed the solar-drive button on his handlebars and launched the MI-TEE Mobile and The Cheesy Rider into the vastness of space.

They were sure to lose Mr. Drools in the King Crab Nebula, just past the Lobsteroid Belt. . . .

17

CHAPTER 2

The Neighbors Are Alien Spies

By Eugene

Eugene and Charlie pedaled their bikes around the block. Most kids would just call it bike riding, but to the members of the Sunnyview Superhero Squad, they were "on patrol."

Evil could lurk anywhere and around any corner. Even in a mailbox! If it was small evil, that is.

The boys turned the corner and Eugene slammed on his brakes. Unfortunately, he stopped too soon, flipped over the handlebars, and landed in a big pile of leaves.

"YAAAAAAAAAAAA!"

"What is it, Eugene?" Charlie said.

"Leaves," Eugene said, holding up a maple leaf. "And a moving van."

Eugene pointed down their street to the end of the cul-de-sac. A moving van was parked in front of the red brick house.

"Maybe they have a kid our age," Charlie said.

"Yeah . . . maybe . . ." Eugene started. "Or maybe it's a house full of aliens, or spies, or . . ."

"ALIEN SPIES!" The two boys shouted out in unison.

Sensing danger, they jumped into the bushes to hide!

"OUCH! PRICKLES!"

Eugene and Charlie jumped back out and hid behind the pile of leaves Eugene had crashed into.

"Do you think they're from a galaxy far, far away?" Charlie asked.

"Aren't all aliens from far away?" Eugene replied.

"What do you think they want?"

Eugene knew *exactly* what they wanted. "Our Super Dude comic books, that's what. Let's get a closer look," he whispered.

"Do you think they have two or four antennae sticking out of their heads?" Charlie was filled with fear and excitement. Antennae sticking out of aliens' heads will do that to a person.

Eugene snuck up the ramp and peeked into the moving van.

"What's inside?" Charlie whispered. "Danger?"

"Furniture."

"Alien spy furniture?"

"Only if alien spies ride bikes," Eugene whispered back.

"Looks like a human bike to me," Charlie said, joining Eugene in the van.

Everything seemed so . . .

NORMAL.

Maybe the aliens are trying to trick the Superhero Squad by pretending to be good guys who "come in peace!" Eugene thought.

"That's a really nice bike, isn't

it?" a mysterious voice asked. An alien spy stood in the doorway, blocking their escape. Eugene and Charlie were cut off!

We're trapped! I fell for the oldest trick in the book: alien spies pretending to be friendly new neighbors who distract me with cool bikes! thought Eugene.

"They don't come in peace, Charlie!" Eugene called out. "They're here to tear us to pieces!"

This alien spy would be no match for Captain Awesome and Nacho Cheese Man!

CHAPTER 3

It's New Kid Monday!

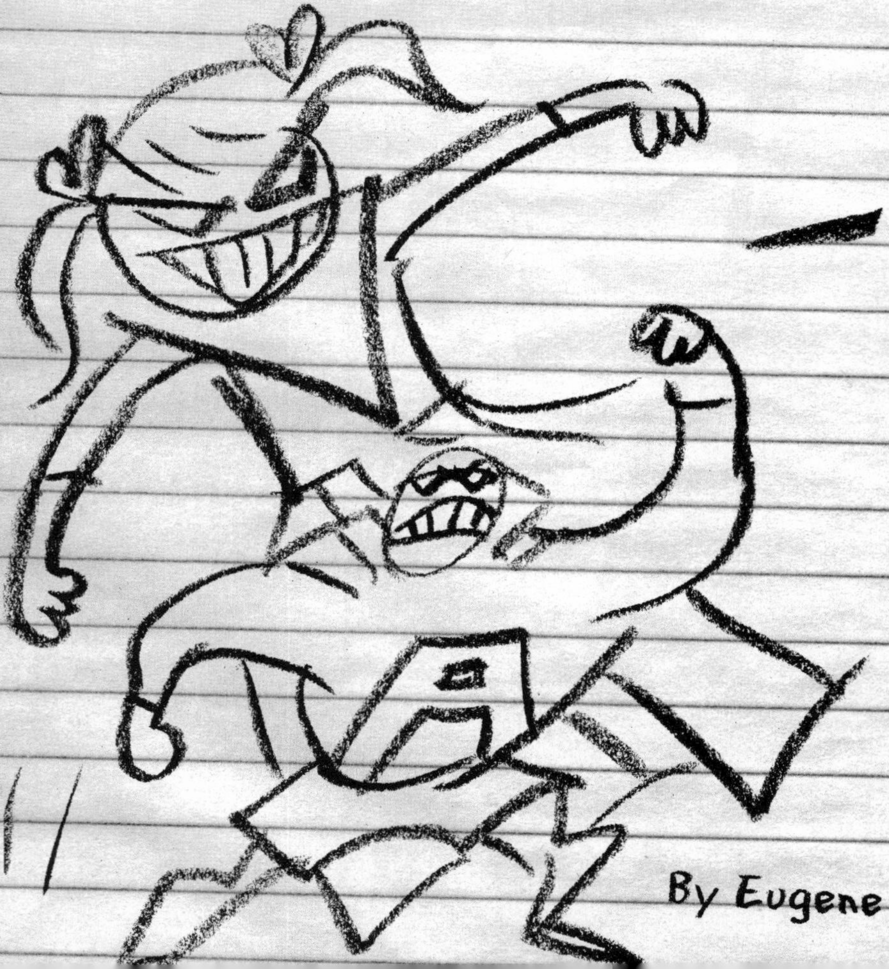

By Eugene

"**C**lass, we have a surprise today," Ms. Beasley said.

It was Monday, which meant Charlie and Eugene were back at school, their superhero uniforms secretly stuffed into their backpacks.

Eugene's eyes lit up when his teacher said "surprise."

What could it be? Pizza Friday is moving to Mondays? We're being sent home early?

Ms. Beasley continued, "Class, say hello to your new classmate Sally Williams."

Everyone was quiet. Even Turbo stopped spinning on his squeaky exercise wheel. The kids stretched their necks like human giraffes to see . . . nothing.

No one was in the doorway.

"WOW! Look! Sally's invisible!" Charlie cried out.

"No, not quite," Ms. Beasley said. "Sally? Would you like to come in and say hello to the class?"

Sally Williams slowly shuffled into the class looking down at her shoes.

Eugene looked down at Sally's shoes too. *Perhaps some villain, like the Incredible Velcrone, had stuck them together!*

Nope.

But her high-top sneakers were so cool that Eugene figured she wanted to look at them as often as she could. Besides, except for the ponytail, the rest of her was dressed just like Eugene and Charlie—a pair of jeans, blue of course, and a T-shirt.

She looked very different from Meredith Mooney. If the color pink ever had a child and sent her to school, she'd look just like Meredith—pink dress, pink socks,

pink shoes, and so many pink ribbons stuck in her hair that it looked like pink meteors had crashed into it.

"Class, let's all say a warm Sunnyview hi to Sally," Ms. Beasley said.

"Hiii, Sal-ly!" the class repeated together.

"Hi," Sally replied, still staring at her shoes, like she was trying to melt them with heat vision.

"Nice shoes," Meredith Mooney said. "For a boy. Is your name Sally Williams . . . or William Sally? That shirt looks like something my brother would wear. Actually, even *he* dresses

better than that. And everyone knows that boys have cooties."

Some of the class giggled.

Hearing the giggles made Meredith continue. "That makes you . . . the COOTIE QUEEN!"

The class roared with laughter, except for Eugene and Charlie. Eugene knew what it was like to be the new kid, and Charlie was too busy counting his cans of spray cheese.

"*Meredith Mooney!*" Ms. Beasley snapped.

Sally's face turned as red as the pickled beets in the cafeteria. She ran past Meredith's desk to an empty seat in the back of the class-room.

Eugene did what heroes do when they see or hear something wrong: HE spoke up.

"Hey! Be quiet! My! Me! Mine! Mere-DITH!" Eugene said. "Every-one knows that the *only* people with

cooties are girls
who wear the
barfy color pink
that's pink like the
color of barf."

The tide shifted and the class
started to laugh at Meredith and
chant, "Pink is barf! Barf is pink!
Pink is barf that makes you stink!"

MI-TEE! Eugene thought. Victory was his! There was no way Meredith could have a comeback for pink barf!

Meredith stuck out her tongue at Eugene.

The ol' Tongue-Stick-Out!? Is that the best she could do? Eugene proudly thought.

"Thank you," Sally whispered so quietly Eugene thought his ears had been stolen.

Eugene whispered, "You're welcome," but Sally was already doodling in her notebook. Eugene sat in his chair, satisfied at his pink, barfy defeat of Meredith and then . . .

WAIT!

Oh . . .

NO!

GROSS!

Eugene felt something crawl up
his arm.

He! Had! **COOTIES!**

It was all part of Meredith's evil cootie plan, for in reality, Meredith Mooney was much more than an annoying little girl who wore too much pink. She was really Captain Awesome's enemy, Little Miss Stinky Pinky!

Even Charlie was scratching the top of his head. He had cooties too!

I say NAY! to you, evildoer!

Eugene thought. *Your evil itchy plan of cootie itchiness will never ever succeed on this day, Little Miss Stinky Pinky! Captain Awesome and Nacho Cheese Man will fight your cooties before they itch again!*

Eugene quickly scratched his left arm.

CHAPTER 4

Peas of Doom and Destruction and YUCK

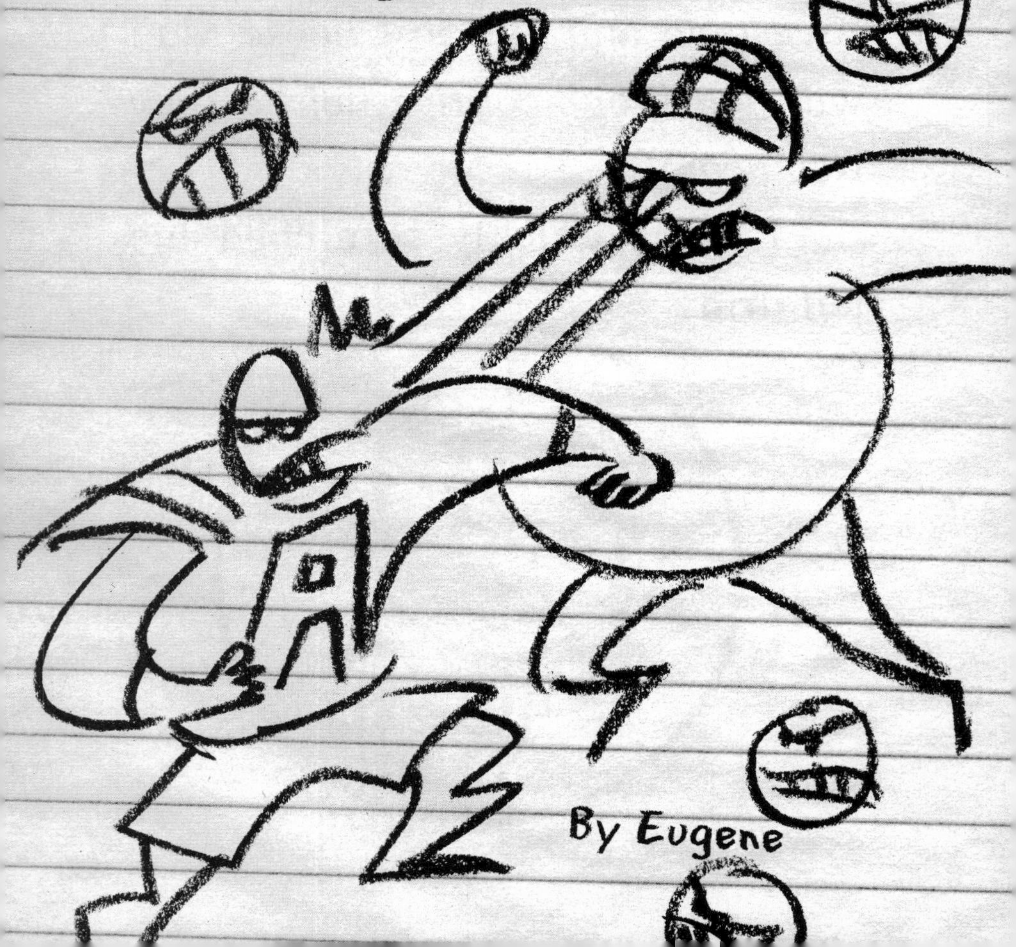

"**N**ow this is our lunch line," Ms. Beasley said to Sally as she proudly pointed out how students get their trays and their forks and wait in line for their food.

Well, DUH.

Eugene wanted to ask Sally to sit with him and Charlie. He remembered his first day at school and how nice it was that Charlie had sat with him.

As a Super Dude fan, Eugene tried to follow Super Dude's "Motto of Niceness" from Super Dude No. 1, No. 15, No. 29, and No. 158: "Being nice is super, so be supernice, dude!"

Before Eugene could say anything to Sally, he smelled a yucky stink! Not the diaper yuck of his nemesis Queen Stinkypants from Planet Baby, but the stinky yuck of another bad guy, the evil cafeteria cook known as **Dr. Spinach!**

Dr. Spinach was a villain so YUCKY, even his first name was

YUCK! Dr. Yuck Spinach.

"Be alert, Nacho Cheese Man," Eugene whispered. "Dr. Spinach is back, and this time, he's brought his most evil round sidekicks . . ."

Charlie gasped. "Noooo! Not. The. Green. Peas!"

"Yes, PEAS!"

"AAAAAAAAAAAAAAAAAA AAAAAAA!" the two boys shouted in unison. You'd think the other kids in the cafeteria would've turned to look, but everyone was pretty much used to Eugene and Charlie shouting AAAAAAAAAAAAAAA AAAAAAAAAA! in the lunch line.

"YUCK! The only vegetable worse than bok choy," Eugene groaned.

Test tubes filled with gravy bubbled behind Dr. Spinach. Pots and pans foamed over with saucy, red Pasta Potions.

"Welcome to the cafeteria, boys!" Dr. Spinach cackled and evilly twirled the ends of his curly, evil mustache.

That's a whole lotta evil, Eugene thought.

With his greasy hairnet and his cackling chicken-laugh, Dr. Spinach was determined to serve Eugene and Charlie his yucky, green, round food of doom!

He knows yucky green peas can steal my Captain Awesome superpowers! thought Eugene.

Professor Beano Greenstalk, in Super Dude No. 19, tried to turn Super Dude into plant food with his slimy Asparagus Ray. But his friends, the Rabbit Rangers from Carrotopia, hopped into battle and kicked Professor Beano Greenstalk right in the cabbage patch. "Never doubt the power of long ears and soft fur," Super Dude said as he tossed Professor Beano Greenstalk onto the compost heap.

Eugene and Charlie had no choice. They'd have to fight their way past Dr. Spinach's Lunch Line of Greasy Terror before he could blast them with school board-approved peas.

"Whatever you do, don't look at him!" Eugene warned. "His Evil Spinach Eyes will zap you!"

CHAPTER 5

The Creature from the Litter Box

LITTER BOX

By Eugene

"Jane has five apples. Jimmy has two more apples than Jane. Karen has one less apple than Jimmy. How many apples does Karen have?"

Where did these kids get all these apples? Eugene wondered. *And why in the world would any kid need six apples?*

But still, homework had to be done. And Eugene was doing it. Until he heard the noise outside his window.

meow.

What was that?

"MEOW." Again.

A cat! At the window! Eugene was instantly suspicious. Was it the Meow Mixer, ready to cough up a Hyper Furball at him?! Or the very bad Katty McKlaw with plans to scratch?! Or *something* WORSE!?

Eugene crept to the window. He threw open the curtains!

"Time to clean your litter box, Katty McKlaw!"

Oh. It was just an ordinary cat on the win- dowsill. Turbo's wheel stopped spinning. Turbo gave the cat a cold stare.

A funny-looking orange cat that looked a lot like orange juice if orange juice had four legs, with little white stripes and green eyes.

"Ew. Peas." The sight of green made Eugene think of the hated vegetable.

Eugene decided right away to call it Funny Cat.

Funny Cat jumped through the open window. Turbo raced to the far edge of his cage and turned his back to the cat with a snort.

Eugene had always wanted a cat . . . and Captain Awesome could use another reliable sidekick, especially one that could use its Claws of

Goodness to catch an evil mouse or climb an evil tree. Eugene rubbed Funny Cat's head.

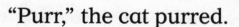

"Purr," the cat purred.

"Aw, mom and dad would never go for another pet." Eugene sighed. As he carried Funny Cat back to the window, a thought popped into his head.

They don't have to know about Funny Cat yet, right?

"I'll bet you have all kinds of awesome cat powers!" Eugene said.

Turbo began running as fast as he could on his wheel.

"Meow," the cat lazily meowed and licked its paw.

"I knew it! You've probably got nine lives and you can always land on your feet!" The possibilities excited Eugene. "Oh! What if Captain Awesome had a cat sidekick . . . oh man! That would totally growl up Mr. Drools!"

Turbo stopped spinning on his wheel and looked right at Eugene.

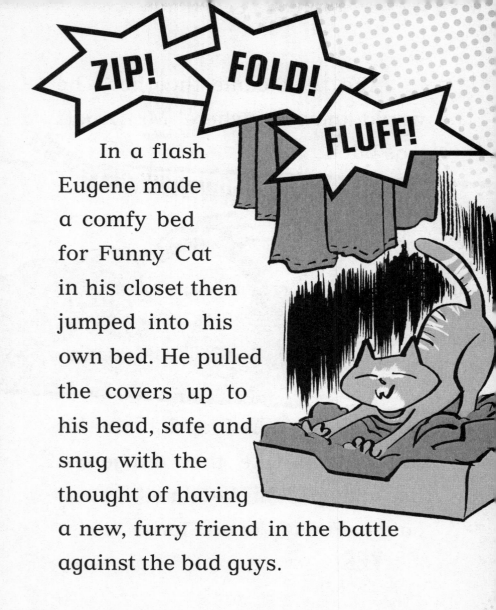

ZIP! **FOLD!** **FLUFF!**

In a flash Eugene made a comfy bed for Funny Cat in his closet then jumped into his own bed. He pulled the covers up to his head, safe and snug with the thought of having a new, furry friend in the battle against the bad guys.

And then came that howl he would know anywhere! Mr. Drools was back!

HOWWWWWWWWWWWL!

Eugene bolted upright in his bed. "Looks like that dangerous dog is up past his bedtime!" Eugene said to Funny Cat and Turbo.

YES!

"Come on, Turbo! Let's introduce Mr. Drools to the newest member of the Sunnyview Superhero Squad! Time to give that tail-wagging do-badder a meowful!"

*S*queak. Squeak. Squeak.

Dr. Yuck Spinach pushed a squeaky cart piled high with boxes of frozen peas down the hall of Sunnyview Elementary.

"Peas, peas, good for your heart! Peas, peas, you'll get a good start! Peas for lunch and peas for dinner! Eat your peas and be a winner!" he sang.

Pure evil!

After Dr. Spinach disappeared into the cafeteria, Eugene and Charlie stepped out from their hiding place behind the bathroom door.

The boys scurried down the hall and outside. Not even evil could make them miss recess.

Sally sat by herself on the steps and quietly

stared at her shoes. Again.

"Hey, what's wrong, Sally?" Eugene said.

Sally burst into tears. "I never wanted to move to Sunnyview! I hate this place! I wanted to stay with my friends! And worst of all," Sally said, "Mr. Whiskersworth has run away."

"Mr. Whiskersworth?" Charlie asked. "Is that your dad?"

"No, my cat."

"What does your cat look like?" Eugene asked.

Sally pulled out a picture of

Mr. Whiskersworth. He was orange, like the color of orange juice if orange juice had four legs, with little white stripes and green eyes.

"Ew. Peas." The sight of green made Eugene think of the hated vegetable.

Mr. Whiskersworth looks just like Funny Cat, Eugene thought. *Maybe they're brothers!*

But before Eugene could say

anything, Sally burst into tears again and ran back into the classroom.

"She's so upset she's going to miss recess?" Eugene said, surprised.

"Wow. I didn't think it was possible to be that upset," Charlie replied.

"This sounds like a job for the Sunnyview Superhero Squad," Eugene said.

The boys were about to leap into action to find the guilty Whiskersworth-napper when a voice called out from the swings behind them.

"We're going to beat you today, Eugene!" It was Mike Flinch.

Bernie Melnik was at his side and stabbed a finger toward the two boys. "Yeah!" Bernie wasn't much of a talker.

Bernie and Mike were both epic

swing jumpers—they could launch themselves off a swing like two elementary school bananas in a slingshot—but could they beat Captain Awesome and Nacho Cheese Man?

"Let Flinch and Melnik beware!" Eugene said.

Intergalactic swing-jumping is one of my many playground super-powers.

Bravely, Captain Awesome and Nacho Cheese Man grabbed their swings and prepared to jump through the rings of Saturn. . . .

CHAPTER 7

Nacho Cheese Man Has a Secret Power You Wish You Had

By Eugene

Was there anything greater than going home from school after such a great victory? Nope. Eugene and Charlie laughed and high-fived all the way home.

Eugene interrupted the happiness with a serious thought. "A cat  that looks *exactly* like Sally's photo of Mr. Whiskersworth came to my room last night. . . ."

"I'll bet it's Mr. Whiskersworth's brother!" Charlie exclaimed.

"I was thinking the *saaaaame* thing," Eugene said. "If only one of us could speak Cat, then we could ask Funny Cat if he knows where Mr. Whiskersworth is!"

"Then it's a good thing one of us *does* speak Cat," Charlie said, then added a meow.

"No. Way."

"Oh yes. Way. I have more than just the power of canned cheese," Charlie said. "I have power over the animals. I can get a dog to come to

me when I call its name. I can pet a dolphin. And I can get a seagull to catch a french fry in midair. Guaranteed!"

Eugene was impressed. *There's a lot more to Nacho Cheese Man than I thought. We'll have to start making a list of our powers!*

"Did you ever wonder how I first discovered Mr. Drools's rotten, no-good plans?"

"Wow! You can read Dog, too?!" Eugene gasped.

"No! Are you nuts?! Every-one knows dogs can't write! But I

can read their doggie minds. Now take me to this cat!" Charlie commanded in his most heroic and commanding voice ever. "But first I gotta ask my mom if I can go over to your house, okay? I think I have piano lessons."

HISS!

Captain Awesome stuck out his hand to pet Funny Cat. "It's okay."

SCRATCH!

"Are you sure he's one of the good guys?" Nacho Cheese Man asked.

Captain Awesome was wondering the same thing. And then he realized the problem!

"Nacho Cheese Man is one of the good guys, Funny Cat! And don't worry, he didn't put a mind-control cheese helmet on my head to make me say that."

"I know what'll convince him." Nacho Cheese Man squirted a bit of cheese onto his finger and held it under the cat's nose. Funny Cat licked the cheese.

"He likes it!" Captain Awesome said.

"Duh. It's cheese." Clearing his throat, Nacho Cheese Man looked into Funny Cat's eyes.

"OMMMMMM!"

he chanted, startling Captain Awesome. "What? It helps me get our brains in tune. OMMMMM!" he chanted again, then leaned closer to Funny Cat. "Funny Cat, where is your brother, Mr. Whiskersworth?" Nacho Cheese Man asked in a commanding voice. He watched Funny Cat lick. "Very interesting . . ."

"What'd he say?" an eager Captain Awesome asked.

"He says he's a cat. And that he loves cheese."

"What about Mr. Whiskersworth?" Captain Awesome asked.

"Oh yeah. I almost forgot." Nacho Cheese Man locked eyes with Funny Cat and in a serious voice

asked, "Do you know where your brother, Mr. Whiskersworth, is?"

There was a short pause as Funny Cat cleaned his whiskers.

"Yes, yes," Nacho Cheese Man said, a bit impatient. "I got that part already. You love cheese. But where is Mr.—"

RUFFFF!

"It's Mr. Drools again!" Captain Awesome yelled. "He's come back for my Frisbee!"

Funny Cat jumped through the open window. He scurried across the roof and climbed down the big maple tree near Eugene's house.

"Wow! Look at Funny Cat go!" Nacho Cheese Man cheered. "The Sunnyview Superhero Squad is right behind you!"

Captain Awesome grabbed Turbo and tucked him into his Turbomobile. "Time to get **MI-TEE!**"

Earth's two greatest heroes not named Super Dude jumped into the teleporter bay and beamed up to the Dog Star to battle the menace of Mr. Drools once more.

Neither hero spoke. This was serious super-hero business. After all, the fate of the world's greatest Frisbee was hanging in the balance.

CHAPTER 9

So the New Neighbor Isn't an Alien Spy After All

By Eugene

"Epic!" Captain Awesome said. His Frisbee was safe again. Mr. Drools had been defeated by the Sunnyview Superhero Squad. "Let doggie-do-badders take note: Not rain nor snow nor too much homework will keep the Sunnyview Superhero Squad from upholding all that is good, right, and . . ."

"Covered in chocolate!" added Nacho Cheese Man.

"Well, I was going to say 'true,' but 'covered in chocolate' isn't bad, either," Captain Awesome admitted.

Captain Awesome picked up Funny Cat. "Ready for a little more mind reading?"

But before Nacho Cheese Man could read any more minds, Funny Cat jumped from Captain Awesome's hands and raced away.

Whoa! I can't lose a cat I just found! thought Eugene.

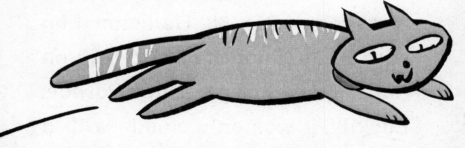

Both Captain Awesome and Nacho Cheese Man took off after Funny Cat. They ran down the side-walk, through Mr. Muckelberry's front yard—he hates when kids do that—jumped over the bushes, and fell into Mrs. Humbert's begonias—she hates when kids do that.

Funny Cat was faster than the lightning from the fingertips of Captain Lightning Fingertips from Super Dude No. 68. He teamed up with King Thunder Toes to rain on Super Dude's Super Dude Parade. Luckily, it was only cloudy with a slight chance of defeat for the bad guys and it was the Super Dudiest parade ever.

Captain Awesome and Nacho Cheese Man screeched to a stop at

the end of the cul-de-sac.

"Uh, Eugene, do you know where we are?"

Funny Cat had led them to the house where the alien spies had just moved in. "We have to get

Funny Cat back before the alien spies hook him up to their alien spy machines and suck out his super-smart cat brain."

"We need a Plan A!" said Nacho Cheese Man.

"And Plans B and C, just in case!"

CRASH!

"What was that?!" said Captain Awesome and Nacho Cheese Man

at the exact same time.

There was no time for any plans, A, B, and certainly not C! It was time for action!

Together Captain Awesome and Nacho Cheese Man ran to the side of the alien spy house where they found four things that each required their own exclamation marks:

1. Sally Williams!

2. Her bike!

3. Trash cans!

4. Funny Cat (sitting on top of the pile, purring and licking his paw like nothing had happened)!

"Are you okay?!" asked Captain Awesome as he helped Sally from the pile of trash cans.

"Mr. Whiskersworth!" Sally was too excited to care about crashing her bike into the trash cans. "You found him!" She looked at the boys in their superhero outfits. "Whoever you're supposed to be."

"I am Captain Awesome!" said Captain Awesome in his most heroic voice ever.

"And I am Nacho Cheese Man," Nacho Cheese Man said, in his most heroic voice ever. He added a heroic pose because you can never be too heroic at times like this.

"We're the Sunnyview Superhero Squad," Captain Awesome explained. "And you're in big danger! This is an alien spy house!"

"Don't be silly," Sally laughed. "This is my house. We just moved in." She gave Mr. Whiskersworth a big, happy squeeze.

Captain Awesome recognized Sally's bike from the moving van. He leaped into action and checked Sally's hair.

"What are you doing?!" Sally said and pulled away.

"Looking for an alien mind-control helmet," Captain Awesome explained, then turned to Nacho Cheese Man. "She's all clear. No alien spyness here."

"Wait a second." A realization hit Nacho Cheese Man. "You called Funny Cat 'Mr. Whiskersworth . . .'"

"Well, *yeah*," Sally hugged the

cat again. "This *is* my cat. See?" Sally showed the boys the cat's collar. It read MR. WHISKERSWORTH.

SHOCK!

"*THAT'S* Mr. Whiskersworth?!" Captain Awesome gasped. He scrunched his nose and looked at Nacho Cheese Man.

"What? I would've figured that out if the cat didn't keep thinking about how much he loved cheese," Nacho Cheese Man said, defending himself.

"He's right! Mr. Whiskersworth does love cheese!" Sally offered.

"See! I knew it! I was right!" Nacho Cheese Man proudly puffed out his chest, then continued, "I bet Mr. Whiskersworth ran away because he was sad that you and your family had to move."

"I was sad to leave too,"

Sally said. "But I'm glad that Mr. Whiskersworth is back."

Captain Awesome was silent. As Sally and Nacho Cheese Man talked, he had a tough decision

to make—even tougher than the time his mom had asked him if he wanted green beans or eggplant with dinner.

Funny Cat belonged to Sally. The duty of any and all super-heroes was to return lost cats to their owners. Even if you really, really, really, like *really*, wanted to keep them for yourself.

Eugene remembered the time that Meredith Mooney hamster-napped poor Turbo. He didn't want to make anyone feel as bad as he had felt on that day.

"Could I have a moment alone with Mr. Whiskersworth?" Captain Awesome asked. Sally handed over her cat and the world's greatest hero who was not named Super Dude gave him a final hug. "I hope you enjoyed being my second sidekick as much as I enjoyed having you as a second sidekick," the

heroic boy whispered into the cat's ear. "Be brave, be good."

"Meow," the cat replied, and Captain Awesome knew that everything would be all right.

"Thanks, Captain Awesome and Nacho Cheese Man, for finding Mr. Whiskersworth. He's my best friend, and I'm so glad he's home." Sally put Mr. Whiskersworth in the basket on her bike. "Now we're going to patrol—I mean *explore* the neighborhood."

"Just be sure to remember to stay out of Mr. Muckelberry's yard,"

Nacho Cheese Man suggested. "He's kinda upset right now." Down the street, Mr. Muckelberry was standing in his front yard, shaking his fist at them.

"We'll go apologize after he's calmed down a little." In his normal Eugene voice, Captain Awesome said to Sally, "I'm glad you got your cat back, Sally. Maybe you'll like Sunnyview more now."

"I think I will."

Sally rode her bicycle down the driveway and into the street. Captain Awesome and Nacho

Cheese Man watched to make sure she used all the proper turn signals. And she did.

"What a great day!" Captain Awesome said.

"Villains bravely defeated, a second sidekick . . . for a while . . . a chase through Sunnyview, and maybe even a new friend to—"

WAIT A MINUTE!

And that was the moment when Captain Awesome saw **IT**.

It was one of the most amazing ITs he had ever, ever seen in, like, forever.

"Check out her bicycle!"

Nacho Cheese Man saw it too! On the back of her seat was a Super Dude license plate.

A Super Dude license plate! SALLY WAS A SUPER DUDE FAN TOO!

"We've really got to get one of those!" Nacho Cheese Man said.

Captain Awesome agreed.

But Captain Awesome couldn't fight the feeling that there was more to Sally than he had originally thought. Could it be that Sally Williams was much more than a mild-mannered girl, new kid on the block, and cat lover? Could it be that she had a power more awesome than just being able to stare at her shoes all day long?

Could it be . . . wondered Captain Awesome. *Could it be that Sally is secretly a superhero, too?*

Sally disappeared around the corner on her bike and Captain Awesome knew his question would just have to wait . . . for now.

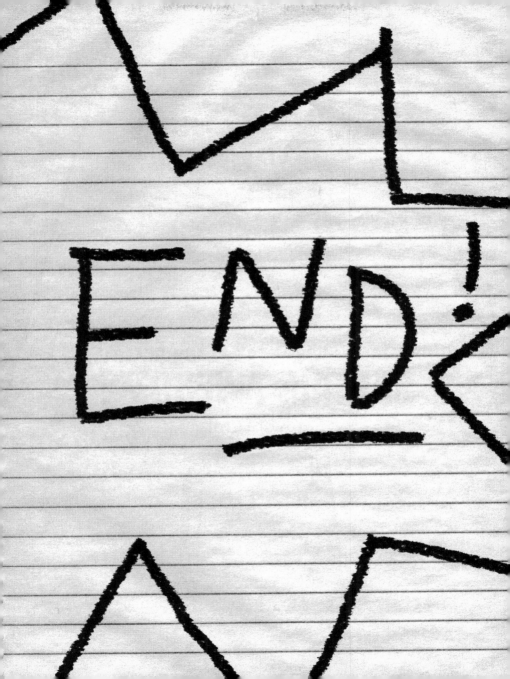

No. 4

CAPTAIN AWESOME
Takes a Dive

BOOM! CRASH! CLANG!

"Evil sounds from the cafeteria!" Charlie gasped.

The boys raced to the cafeteria, flung open the doors, and saw truly yucky evil.

The two boys dove for cover.

"It's our old enemy, Dr. Yuck Spinach!" Eugene whispered.

"He must have escaped from Asteroid Prison and returned to continue his evil vegetable plans!"

"There's only one way out of this veggie trap," Eugene said. "Make a direct charge through

Dr. Spinach's evil Cafeteria Lair."

"That's insane!" Charlie gasped. "We'll never make it! He'll use his Okra Bombs and Asparagus Spears!"

"Yes. And his Poison Parsnips, too," Eugene replied. "But Super Dude never says 'Never!'"

It's time for action!

"CHAAAAARGE!" he shouted and raced into the cafeteria!

BOUNCE!

Oops!

Eugene tripped over the doorway and flopped to the floor.

ROLL!

Turbo's plastic ball flew from Eugene's hands and rolled across the cafeteria floor . . . stopping at Dr. Spinach's feet.

"EEEPS!" Charlie gasped in horror as Dr. Spinach turned to pick Turbo up.

"What have we here?" the evil chef of leafy green yuckiness growled.

Eugene and Charlie yanked their costumes from their backpacks.

When **STAN KIRBY** was six years old, he tied a beach towel around his neck and became Super Commander Beach Boy. He tried his best to protect sand castles from the waves, keep seagulls away from his french fries, and keep the beach clean. When Stan's not creating the awesome adventures of Captain Awesome, he loves reading comic books, eating okra, and hang gliding (but not at the same time).

GEORGE O'CONNOR'S cover—as a mild-mannered clerk in one of Gotham's most beloved children's bookstores—was completely blown when his first picture book, *KAPOW!*, exploded onto the scene. Forced to leave the bookselling world behind, he now spends even more time in his secret Brooklyn, New York, hideout—where he uses his amazing artistic powers to strike fear in the hearts of bad guys everywhere!